ARMED WITHOUT BIBLES

LINDSAY BROWN

LifeRich PUBLISHING®

LifeRich Publishing is a registered trademark of
The Reader's Digest Association, Inc.

LifeRich Publishing books may be ordered through booksellers or by contacting:

LifeRich Publishing
1663 Liberty Drive
Bloomington, IN 47403
www.liferichpublishing.com
844-686-9607

Because of the dynamic nature of the Internet, any web addresses or
links contained in this book may have changed since publication and
may no longer be valid. The views expressed in this work are solely those
of the author and do not necessarily reflect the views of the publisher,
and the publisher hereby disclaims any responsibility for them.

This is a work of fiction. All of the characters, names, incidents,
organizations, and dialogue in this novel are either the products
of the author's imagination or are used fictitiously.

Any people depicted in stock imagery provided by Getty Images are
models, and such images are being used for illustrative purposes only.
Certain stock imagery © Getty Images.

ISBN: 978-1-4897-3075-6 (sc)
ISBN: 978-1-4897-3076-3 (hc)
ISBN: 978-1-4897-3092-3 (e)

Library of Congress Control Number: 2020918071

Print information available on the last page.

LifeRich Publishing rev. date: 09/14/2020

To my husband and three children, who inspire me

to write stories that arrive as gifts from God.

For as many as are led by the Spirit of

God, they are the sons of God.

—Romans 8:14

CONTENTS

CHAPTER 1

TOUGH TIMES

A war begins in the year 2020 between the United Countries (UC) and the United Alliance of the Anti-Knowing (UAAK). Global political upheavals shock citizens. Fear permeates lawless cities around the world. Roaming gangs, peacekeepers, looters, and individuals seeking clean water, food, and energy threaten local survivors. Crooked financiers confiscate businesses wrecked by conflict. Property scalpers seek properties to sell on the black market. Carnal bartering is rampant. Dignity is shelved as coarse survival strategies darken souls. The death of parents gives birth to peculiar persons, neither children nor adults.

The UAAK's military, the U-Squad, create a nuclear attack system undetectable by the UC. Due to critical losses in the year 2023, the UAAK decides to end the war. Tired and without financial support from allies, the UAAK pushes a fatal button, raising hell to earth. Explosions erupt. Plumes of smoke and vermillion flame fog skylines. The earth grows cold and pitch black. Survivors call this environment "Entity." The darkness feels like an invisible villain killing horribly, silently, and quickly. Surviving mothers suffer double pain: despair over the desolation and the excruciating deaths of children. Strange new illnesses pervade the world without remedy. Regions lack doctors or medicine to help the millions languishing from radiation poisoning. The war ends. Or does it?

The UAAK and allies organize a new government, where lunacy is dressed in scholarly prose, good is reviled as evil, and evil is embraced as good. Politicians stake their false flags in imaginary ground. Things once sacred like freedom of speech, the right of assembly, life, liberty, and the pursuit of happiness are forbidden under the rule of the UAAK. Freedom of the press becomes nothing more than a rumor after politically incorrect speech riots spread. The proud fists of feminists lower as women are returned to a status of submission they thought the Equal Rights Amendment had abolished. "PG" (Property of the Government) is tattooed on the forehead of those captured among the ashes. Materials, both digital and corogital, a new technology, are singularly controlled. Ruling philosophy dictates the confiscation of contraband materials, particularly materials that are religious in nature, including text remaining on singed pages that children scribbled.

Forced underground are the Followers of the All-Knowing (FAK). FAKs develop a secret network to give those willing to listen an opportunity for hope through the All-Knowing. The All-Knowing is believed to be a dangerous myth. Tattered fabrics used as doors are pulled closed at the mention of FAKs—not because of their behavior but because the neogovernment does not tolerate them. FAK screams fill the air during timed executions. Torture is timed to terrorize listening ears. Seized FAK leaders undergo a series of psychological tests, unknown to them, to identify their worst fear before they are executed.

Seven families have organized and run the FAK network. The state searches vehemently for the leaders of this network. "Eradicate Religion" is one of the UAAK's fight songs. FAK acts of civil and spiritual disobedience threaten the government. Among the UC, six FAK families have been located. Their fate is in the hands of a snapping hydra government, and an execution order is issued.

CHAPTER 2

---◦---

OUR STORY BEGINS

Washington, DC, lacks the activity and trust it once enjoyed. The halls of justice are now dim and gloomy due to ruin of war and rampant suicide. Justice wears a tilted mask with holes. The government, once caretaker of the soul of the nation, now facilitates human vices. Abortions are readily available. Many babies who survive abortions are executed when their mothers give the thumbs-up to death. Rapacious sexual desires lead to untold acts. The government is a drug and drug paraphernalia vendor. Addicts are the flora of parks, benches in subways, and paths for sidewalks.

In an interior room of a court building, a judgment is decreed. Six couples will be killed by lions and thrown into a smoldering furnace. "We'll find out if what you believe will save you," a grotesque judge shouts. The twelve of them stand silent, eyes fixed on the judge, who sits elevated in a mahogany bench with ornate relief. They are escorted from the court, taken into a room, and stripped. The men and women gaze away from each other.

"Where are you taking us?" the oldest woman asks.

"To the lions. You die today!" one guard spits.

"That's rather dramatic," one of the women says.

The twelve utter prayers. Nude, they are transported to a zoo, where they are thrust into a lions' den. Lions slowly climb from rocks toward the FAKs. The six men lock hands with their wives standing behind them, quietly resigned. "May this be our swan song," a man bellows. "Loving, All-Knowing God, let us suffer this painful death alone. Let our wives sleep now, for only You know the why and the how."

In unison the men yield to the violence of the lions while repeating part of the ancient text: "Through glory and dishonor, bad report and good report; genuine, yet regarded as impostors; known, yet regarded as unknown; dying, and yet we live on."

The women reach to touch their husbands one last time but faint onto the den floor. Suddenly, sharp, long teeth and strong jaws bite and rip their tender flesh. The den is wet and bloody. Screams and the sounds of lions savagely eating cause some guards to wince and a nearby zookeeper to regurgitate. News of the deaths travels rapidly through the underground.

CHAPTER 3

THE CALL

Antonio, the son of a fallen leader, weeps with his sisters, Alessandra and Maria, and Aunt Ruth in his family's sitting room in Bulia, Italy. Lush curtains cover the floor-to-ceiling windows. Walls boast mahogany wainscoting and antique gold wallpaper with just a touch of flocking. Filled with sliding doors, wall pockets, doorknob lighting fixtures, hidden rooms, a room without a ceiling, and an invisibility closet, the inherited house is a beloved family member. The family's slogan is "You either love the house or hate the house."

"Please, stop this crying, sisters. Mama and Papa died as martyrs. It is well with them. The All-Knowing is pleased," Antonio says calmly as he dries his eyes.

"How can you talk of the All-Knowing? He has caused your parents to be killed like common criminals," Aunt Ruth replies.

"You don't understand. How long will your vision be obscured?" Antonio says.

His aunt is vehement. "This is a miserable day! Good people murdered, and for what? For being followers of the All-Knowing!"

Antonio responds somberly. "Do not whisper. I am not ashamed."

His oldest sister Alessandra pipes up. "Aunt, Antonio is right. It is a time to rejoice. Papa and Mama are with the All-Knowing. They don't have to hide or go hungry or worry—" She bursts into tears and covers her face with her hands. "I'm sorry, I miss them so. My whole body aches!"

Aunt Ruth offers her a handkerchief from her dress pocket. Alessandra wipes her eyes and nose.

"I'm better now. Papa's work is unfinished," Alessandra says.

"I cannot work. I am exhausted," Aunt Ruth replies.

"Come, Auntie, I will help you to your room. You'll feel better after some rest," Maria, Antonio's youngest sister, says as she and Aunt Ruth leave the room.

"Brother, as I was saying, there is much work to be done. The Anti-Knowing is much stronger in the United Soviet States overseas. People there are not accustomed to repression and being murdered for breaking rules that were once freedoms of habit," Alessandra says.

"I know. I must pray to the All-Knowing for guidance. With Papa's death, there is no leader to fight against the Anti-Knowing. Let me think on it awhile. For now, we should rest," Antonio says.

"Good night, Antonio." Alessandra squeezes her brother's hand before retiring up the stairs to her bedroom.

Antonio wakens in the middle of the night and jumps out of bed. He walks to his closet and rushes into gray khaki pants and a houndstooth shirt. Worn black loafers lay below the window, and a brown leather pilot's jacket hangs from a hook on the wall. His dark hair and amber eyes shine violently in the moonlight, which peers through a crack in the window curtain. He walks down the stairs and out the front door of the house. His aunt, weary with insomnia, watches him from her bedroom window.

Antonio takes a flying train to a struggling but not dilapidated area. While riding, Antonio is thankful that this area wasn't as hard hit by the war as some others. Most homes are simple and still livable. He is also glad his family members—Alessandra, Maria, and Aunt Ruth—are safe at home. He departs from the train and walks down the street to an old, well-kept building. He knocks on the door but gets no response. He knocks again, and the door slowly opens, a chain catching it.

Timeworn periwinkle eyes peep through. "What is your business, young man?" the woman asks.

"My name is Antonio," he says.

The chain rattles as the door opens quickly. "Please

come in. He has been waiting for you. Follow me," the woman says in an endearing voice.

They walk down a lengthy, dimly lit corridor, portraits on either side. An old, faded stained-glass window is at the center end of the corridor. Walking in silence, they approach a door on the right wall.

"In here," the woman says as she opens the door.

Antonio scans the modest bedroom. Perplexed, he says, "Ma'am, I don't believe you understand—"

"Open the closet door, step in, and find your way. Don't be afraid. I'll be sitting here waiting for you," she interrupts.

Antonio hesitates, then steps in. Clothes hang in the closet. He sorts through them to find an opening. No knobs, handles, switches—nothing. He wonders whether it's a trap. He peers out the door, somewhat frustrated; he hunches his shoulders and raises his hands.

"The entrance is protected by Him. Ask Him to guide you. If you are who you say you are, you will find your way," he hears her say.

13

He closes the closet door, stands erect with head bowed humbly, and quietly prays, "Lord, I have been sent by You. Lead me." He opens his eyes and touches a panel in the closet; the wall opens. He goes through.

The old woman sits knitting in the chair; the room is intact. Antonio walks cautiously down the dark, musky staircase. He sees an old man sitting at a plain wooden table, with a dingy blue lamp hanging overhead. He wears a grimy shirt covered by a worn vest. He beckons to Antonio. Antonio walks to the table and pulls out a chair.

"I'm glad you have come. We must get started. The forces of darkness are rejoicing. I am certain that no one will oppose them," the old man says.

"No one?" Antonio says.

"No man or woman. Enough chatter. Let me explain why you're here. There is a battle being waged against the All-Knowing by the Anti-Knowing. Although there are physical casualties, it is not a battle of flesh and blood but instead of the spiritual sort," the old man explains.

"My father taught me much about the enemy and encouraged me not to fear," Antonio reassures.

The old man continues. "It will take a strong heart. There are six other children like yourself. You have been taught in the ways of discipline and of love for the All-Knowing. There are children who know we are engaged in spiritual warfare, but they do not know they are soldiers in this war."

The old man lifts a brow and looks directly at Antonio. Antonio swallows and listens intently. "I envision that you seven children will fight against and win the battle over these evil forces," the old man portends.

CHAPTER 4

LEAVING HOME

O n the way home, Antonio notices he is being followed someone weaving in and out of the shadows. He can't see the face but believes it is a man; however, it could be a woman or a transgender person. A half a block away, the Burr Ridge train station sign hangs above the heads of passing pedestrians. At the station, curving and shrinking his shoulders, Antonio boards the flying train. Scanning the train, he locates a seat in the rear right corner. Antonio sits. He grabs his head, rubbing it rapidly. He sees a band tightening around his head as an Anti-Knowing force penetrates his mind and streams demonic videos.

"Ugh!" he shouts in pain.

Passengers turn toward the sound. "What's wrong with you?" asks a passenger standing near him.

Antonio looks up. It is the face he couldn't make out on the street. "It's nothing," he manages to speak.

"You're still holding your head," the passenger says.

"Sometimes I get headaches," Antonio says.

"From where I'm standing, it looks as though an aervio—you know, an aerial violent video— band projection mirrored from a distance entered your mind," the passenger says.

Still holding his head, Antonio grimaces at the passenger. "A what?" he asks in pain.

Reaching toward him, the passenger touches Antonio between his brows. Flashing on Antonio's inward eye is a warm, golden liquid that dissolves the tight band. Antonio slowly releases his head.

Looking at the passenger, Antonio exclaims, "That's extraordinary!"

"Learn to stop unwanted things from entering your mind," the passenger says.

Antonio asks, "What did you—"

A buzzing sound interrupts him. "Hold on. I need to answer this." Antonio turns away to answer the text on his cell. As he turns back to complete his sentence, the passenger is gone. Walking to the front of the train, Antonio pauses at each seat, looking for the mysterious stranger.

No one resembling the stranger is on the train.

Antonio returns to his seat and gazes out of the window. After deplaning, he remains in the boarding area, still looking. "Sir, everyone is off the train," an attendant says.

Antonio takes a taxi home. As he enters the kitchen, the smell of pungent garlic arouses his nostrils. His aunt stands over the stove, stirring a pot of boiling deliciousness. "Antonio, where did you go so early?" Aunt Ruth inquires.

"I had to look after Father's business," he says.

"Oh. Most places of business are not open so early," she says.

"Why do you question me?" Antonio says as he turns his back to his aunt.

"Because you have been acting strangely since the death of your parents," Aunt Ruth pleads.

Antonio turns toward her. "Aunt, it is the living who need caring," he conveys with a wisdom beyond his years.

"Yes, without a doubt," she agrees. "I, too, am concerned with the living. Have you eaten?"

"No, I'm not hungry," he says flatly, walking away and disappearing into his bedroom.

Meanwhile, Claudio, captain of the local legislature destroyer team, speaks to his battalion. "We have done well. Twelve of our enemies are gone. This will be a lesson to others who think the All-Knowing can help them."

A soldier calls out, "Captain, why were these twelve All-Knowing killed?"

The captain is incensed. "Questions! Do I hear a

question about the All-Knowing? What are you? A follower?" Claudio shouts.

"No, Captain, I just—"

"You just sealed your fate, cadet! You'll be a lesson to the men." Claudio draws his flasher and fires. The soldier falls dead. Claudio smiles as he looks down at the dead cadet and looks back up seriously at the remaining battalion. "Questions will not be tolerated." He returns his flasher to its holster and swaggers out of the room.

In horror, the men look at each other in fearful sorrow. "He was a good man. He had a family!" a solider cries as his fallen friend is lifted from the floor. Perspiration and fear mingle in the air, creating a dense tension that weighs heavily on the men.

Several counties over, Antonio yells, "Oww-ow!" while grasping his head in his hands. He falls to the floor on his knees. His head feels as though it is sliding through a pasta dough machine. Pictures are forming in his head, but he struggles to hold them.

Relax, a voice reverberates from inside his head. He lowers his arms and breathes deeply. The pain fades.

He sees a boy. The boy appears far off. As Antonio focuses, he notices that the boy is asking him to come to him. His mind captures the picture in his head. The Himers Institute is what the sign reads. The Institute doesn't have a fence around it. It's surrounded by a lush, green property with a beautiful landscape.

The boy signals him. *Come this way.*

Antonio gets up from the floor and meanders toward his bed. When he flops down, the covers become disarrayed. He lies back on the bed, staring at the ceiling. Cracks and peeling paint look back at him. He wonders when it was painted last and where the Himers Institute is. The boy in his head seemed so real.

A voice calls from the corridor while someone knocks lightly on the door. "Antonio? Are you in there?"

Straightening his hair, Antonio gets up and opens the door. "Alessandra, what's wrong?"

"We heard you cry out. We're worried about you," Alessandra responds.

"I came into my room, and my head began to hurt. The excruciating pain forced me to my knees. I didn't mean to alarm you." He knows he can't tell them he is seeing things, hearing things, that aren't there. They might consider him unbalanced.

Antonio turns away from Alessandra and walks toward the dresser. He fidgets with the rock in his pocket. "Alessandra, I need to be alone. I'll eat later," Antonio tells her, and she leaves the room.

Antonio leaves behind her, unnoticed. He makes his way to his father's library, somewhat disoriented, hoping to find information on the Himers Institute. Once he is inside the library, his grief overwhelms him, and the absence of his father's life force strikes his heart. The trashed books, Venetian lamps in the corner of the room, a massive golden globe to the left of the desk, the cracked foot soldiers, the lion statues (now destroyed), and strewn papers are all that are left of the violent, thorough search the U-Squad performed.

Aunt Ruth had told him that after his parents were seized, the U-Squad stormed the house. "What were they looking for?" Antonio had asked Aunt Ruth. "I should have helped father more," he remembers saying as he slumps into his father's chair, a large, well-worn leather chair he can't fill.

I can't do this, I just can't. I've never fought for anything or put myself in harm's way. Now I'm asked to find people I don't know and lead them. I am no leader. This must be some crazy nightmare. I am the naive child of two zealots. I want my father's arm of protection before me. This is just too great, and it all must be done in secrecy. What about money? Money? What about Claudio and his men? What about Auntie Ruth, Alessandra, and Maria? What about the All-Knowing? Just how deep am I into this?

His eyes scan the library. He notices a bookcase that is unequally aligned. Hours pass as he searches through the case; he finds nothing. Tired, frustrated, and hungry, he continues to search for the smallest clue to proceed.

Why did I expect to find anything here? The U-Squad left the library looking like firefighters were tearing out the walls, trying to find a hidden ember. Yet I believe father must have left some sort of clue, but where?

Dumf, dumf, dumf!

There are rumbles outside the front of the house.

Antonio jumps to his feet, stalks to the library door, and peers through the sliver of an opening, straining to see around the wall edges.

Maria approaches. "Aunt Ruth thinks that it's the U-Squad. You'd do well to hide," she whispers. Antonio waves Maria into the library.

"Agh! You can't just barge in here!" Aunt Ruth screams.

Two soldiers enter the home, looking around. "We can, and we have! Anybody else here with you?" one soldier asks.

"Just my nieces," she answers.

One soldier draws his flasher and walks close to Aunt Ruth. Slowly she backs ups and breaks eye contact. A misshapen clump of scar tissue forms an ugly pile below the soldier's right eye near his nose. She recoils, holding tightly to her collar. She is repulsed by those gray uniforms. Everything appears gray to her now.

"No one else," she repeats firmly.

In the library, Antonio gestures to Maria, "I must leave. Tell the others not to worry. I will contact you when I can." Antonio sneaks out of the library, unseen and unheard. Afraid that the U-Squad are seeking to arrest him, Antonio steps into the deep darkness; unaware of his future, he goes for the only help he knows—the old man.

Just as before, Antonio takes a flying train, and just as before, he feels he is being followed by a stranger weaving in the shadows of night. As he approaches the building of the old man, he looks about timidly to see whether he's still being followed. It appears safe, so he proceeds.

"I'm coming. Stop ringing the bell!" calls a voice from

behind the door. A familiar well-worn face peers at him. "Why are you here? The rocks did not glow," the old woman says.

"Pardon?" Antonio shuffles his feet nervously. "I need help. The U-Squad are at my house. I think they're looking for me. But before the U-Squad arrived, a boy called to me from some kind of dream state. I need to see the old man. I can't go home now. I need help to go forward."

"Shh-hh!" the old woman says while removing the chain and unlocking the door. "Very well then, go in," she says.

Antonio enters the closet and goes into the basement. The basement is unlit. "Hello. Anyone here?" he calls out.

"It's me, Antonio." A spent matchstick sounds. Light from a lantern reveals an old man walking toward him. "I was not expecting you so soon."

"Tonight two U-Squads came to my house, and prior to that, a boy called to me in a vision. I believe he is at the Himers Institute." Excitedly, Antonio continues. "Do you know of this place? And how is he able to enter my mind? Who is he?"

"Come sit down. I had hoped that time was on our side, but it looks as though we have no time to lose," the old man says. "Are you ready?"

"It appears that I, like my parents, have no choice," Antonio says.

"This boy that called to you. He can speak telepathically. All of the children you must locate have special abilities," the old man says, looking directly at Antonio.

Antonio breaks his gaze, looking toward the jar of lemon drops on the table. He didn't want to seem rude, but he could taste the tart white powder of the wrapper and the sweet candy it covered.

"Take as many as you like," said the old man, pushing the jar to Antonio.

"Thank you. I am famished," Antonio says. He removes the lid and pops two candies into his mouth, his stomach growling madly.

"As I was saying, all the children have special gifts. Let me see ... the gifts are charity, faith, fighting—no, not fighting—but one is valiant, discernment. Wait ... now what was the other one?" He scratches his balding head in an attempt to remember. "Oh yes, I have it—an ability to heal and psychic ability," the old man recalls.

"What then is my gift?" Antonio asks.

"That you must discover for yourself," the old man answers. "You can stay here for the night. I will have Inez bring you food to calm the outcry in your belly. Tomorrow you begin your journey," he says, climbing the stairs.

Alone in the basement, Antonio takes a good look around. Several catacomb corridors are visible. Antonio wonders where they lead and whether others are in the basement. Light casts a narrow triangle in the room as the basement door opens. Antonio notices that for his age, the old man spryly descends the stairs. "I had hoped that you got a chance to study the writings given to you earlier, but there was no way of knowing today's events," the old man says. "Inez prepared this for you."

A large blue bowl is placed before Antonio. He licks his lips as he inserts a spoon into the red sauce that covers steaming ravioli pasta.

The old man smiles. "Fear makes some hungry. Others it grips and takes everything from them, even their appetite. But clearly not you." He chuckles.

Antonio blushes.

The old man continues, "I will make a place for you over here. You should be comfortable."

"Thank you," Antonio mumbles through a mouth full of pasta.

During the night, Antonio falls into a heavy sleep. His eyes dart about frantically. Emotional images appear and disappear in rapid succession. In one dream, he is looking for the boy, who calls to him. He sees blue skies, white puffy clouds, and green meadows.

His parents appear. Their arms are stretched toward him in the distance, and he runs to hug them.

Suddenly, the landscape turns ominous. Serenity is replaced by darkness, and gray smoke makes it difficult to breathe. A grotesque flying gargoyle swoops down from a once-beautiful mountain, between him and his parents.

"Ahh!" Antonio screams. The creature reaches for

him. His parents throw large, heavy rocks at the creature, diverting its attention.

"#@#%^*%$#@!" the creature wails.

Antonio's parents run and hide behind a large boulder. When they close their eyes and concentrate, an invisible magnetic field stops the creature from advancing farther.

"Save yourselves!" Antonio screams to his parents. "Run! Run now! Run!" he pleads.

The loud noise breaks his parents' concentration. The gargoyle's calloused, clawed feet snatch up his parents like field mice. They look like worms being used as bait. The gargoyle ties them down with branches from a nearby tree. Antonio runs and slides to quickly hide behind a bush.

"Where are you?" the gargoyle snarls as he searches around for Antonio. "Come out! I will find you! Your fear is leading me to you."

"Don't be afraid, don't be afraid, don't be afraid," Antonio coaches himself. As the creature comes closer, Antonio bravely stands firm and, using a sling made from his undershirt, hurls the rock from his pocket.

"Humph," mumbles the creature as his wound smolders.

Antonio sprints away with knees rising and lowering from his chest. Suddenly, the sky appears darker and close to his head. A quick glance upward reveals a reptile foot attached to twelve-inch toenails about to flatten him.

His parents work feverishly to get loose.

"Oh God! Help me!" Antonio screams. He lies

positioned for the coroner's chalk; there is a crushing weight on his chest. Fear perforates his entire body; his heart beats wildly.

Suddenly, he gasps for air and realizes he's sweating in his bed. "I'm alive! It was only a dream!" he says aloud, relieved. He settles himself and thinks it was good to see his parents alive. "'Our father, who art in heaven. Hallowed be thy name … thy kingdom … come,'" he whispers as he falls back to asleep. Unbeknownst to Antonio, light resides near him as he sleeps. The next morning comes quickly.

"Sleep well?" the old man asks.

"Oh yes. I could get used to being stomped by gargoyles," Antonio says sarcastically.

"Be faithful. You woke up, didn't you? Never allow yourself to die in your dream," the old man remarks.

"What do you mean?" Antonio asks, confused.

"Battles fought in the sleep world could be a dream or could not be," the old man explains. Shaking a finger at Antonio, he continues, "So whatever you do, don't die there. We need you here."

"I hit the creature with the rock Inez gave me. It burned the gargoyle's flesh, yet it wasn't hot or cold in my pocket," Antonio says.

"Rocks are used to communicate. Inez and others can focus energy into the rock. If we need you to come here or to contact us, the rock will change color. Followers of the All-Knowing can use the energy in many ways just by engaging our intention. Hold onto the rock. Use it wisely," the old man says.

"What's your name?" Antonio asks.

"It is better you do not know. Should you be captured, you can honestly say I know no one by that name. Truth will save you. Marry her," the old man says. He turns his back to Antonio and clears papers from the top of a hand-carved wooden cabinet. Antonio knows it is hand carved because his mother especially liked custom woodwork.

"I'm going to call you 'Luca.' I can't go on calling you

'an old man,'" Antonio says, tucking his shirt into his trousers and neatening his hair.

"You call me an old man?" the old man asks with hurt pride.

"Not really. I haven't talked to anyone about you, but I think it fits you," Antonio explains, walking toward the old man.

"Well, perhaps that's true." The old man chuckles. "Did you study any last night?"

"No, but I am anxious to get underway."

"Good, sit here," he says, motioning Antonio toward the chair.

"Okay, Luca, but I need to pray first," Antonio says as he bows his head and quietly prays.

Roughly pushing Antonio's hands down, the old man quips, "I have not given you permission to call me 'Luca.'"

"What are you doing?" Antonio asks.

"You cannot pray like that. You will get yourself killed!" the old man shouts at Antonio, looking around, paranoid. "Pray like this." The old man stands, still looking straight ahead.

"It doesn't look like you're praying," Antonio says.

"Exactly! Now be seated," the old man says. Antonio obeys.

"Death and her friends, destruction and woe, will be on your heels. You must be wise and watchful. Consider every move you make if you are to successfully lead the other six," the old man says. "You have to be a full-grown man now."

Rubbing his hands nervously, Antonio assures him, "I am watchful. Death has been following me. I gave him the slip after I got off the train."

"That wasn't death! You're alive," the old man says. "Did the being following you wear an oversized navy military coat and a dark hat? Did he walk with his head down?"

Antonio nods.

"Then you should know—you have a Guardian," the old man says.

Antonio stands up. "I have a Guardian?"

"Yes, you do. However, even he can't fully protect you. You must be wise and cunning. Your enemies will seek to distract your Guardian, which is why you must locate the other six children. Seven is the number of perfection and completion. For you seven is also a number of power and protection. You will watch each other's backs."

"Is that what happened to our parents ... their Guardians were distracted?" Antonio asks with his eyes welling up. "We're kids. How am I supposed to lead six kids when twelve adults were unsuccessful?"

"Negative energy must be controlled. You can get angry, but it must be righteous anger. The Anti-Knowing track negative energy. They can identify all negative energy patterns associated with their members. If your temper is unleashed, an undocumented energy marker will appear on their radar, and they will seek to locate it. The Anti-Knowing will find you. Enough talk. Let's get to work."

Breathing in, Antonio oxygenates every cell in his body and commands it to attention. Eyes fixed on the turning pages before him, the old man points to places on maps and describes secret corridors, escape passages, passwords for safe harbor. Antonio listens. Like an anteater sucking in its prey, Antonio captures every idea, date, address, and name.

Sparks fly out of his inner eye, sensing something quirky about to happen. He looks even more intently at the old man as he masks his father's 3D image, whispering, "Remember, fear is only a distracter." The image vanishes.

"Has the network helped kids before?" Antonio asks.

"There was no need. The network was run by adults— your parents and others like them," the old man says.

"I'm summoning my wits. I believe I can find the other six. Who's the fairy in the woods?"

"Have you seen Rita?" the old man asks eagerly.

"Yes, just now. She and a black kid with red curly hair and blue eyes invaded my thoughts. Weird." He squirms.

"Rita is no fairy. She's a TD," the old man says.

"A TD? What's a TD?" Antonio asks.

"Tree Dweller," the old man says smartly. "The black kid, as you call him, is named Magus. It is he who is sending you the images. He's probably picking up on your thoughts, even though he has never met Rita. Back to work. We need to work on your clothes. You need to look less put together."

CHAPTER 5

JOURNEY TO UNKNOWN PLACES

A light breeze blows trash in Antonio's path. He looks down and notices the trash oddly circling. He bends to take a closer look and loses his footing. Feeling intense weight collapse his forearm, Antonio struggles to see beyond his oversized hoodie.

"Ahh!" he shrieks, landing on his backside. The circling trash dances about him. His bruised hand and scraped knuckles fail to break his fall.

"You okay?" a voice asks.

Rising to his feet, Antonio wipes his swelling hand across his pants. He asks, "Why did you pull me into this alley?"

"I pulled you in," the stranger says. "You, sir, are clumsy. Don't blame me for your fall."

Antonio frowns at the stranger.

"First things first, I need to talk to you. And second, I am Ian Smith." He extends his hand to Antonio. "I know you, and I can help you," Ian Smith says.

Flexing his throbbing knuckles, Antonio sizes up Ian Smith. Ian Smith's lavender front- fitted blazer has an interesting double-peak collar lapel, the top collar an inch shorter than the lower collar, with black piping on the jacket pockets and sleeve bottoms. Running from collar to seam on the jacket's back is a single ruffle, which is barely noticeable. The black back of the blazer and black jeans contrast with the blazer's front and white-tailored shirt.

Are those alligator penny loafers? Antonio wonders.

Antonio tells Ian, "I don't need any help from someone who violently yanked me into an alley."

"What's with you and old news? I dislike repeating myself," Ian Smith says. "Just to be sure, you are Antonio, right? Though I almost didn't recognize you in this costume," he says, pointing to Antonio's outfit."

"Who's asking?" Antonio responds.

Ian Smith's face reddens. "Once again, I am Ian Smith. The state killed your parents, correct?"

"Your name tells me nothing of who you are," Antonio says.

"I am employed by the Himers Institute," Ian Smith replies, handing Antonio a dark, golden card.

Flipping the card over and shrugging, Antonio reads, "Himers Institute."

"It's di-gi-tal! Put it in your pocket. Come on, the commander wants to meet you." Ian Smith guides Antonio down the alley.

"Commander?" Antonio asks.

"Our leader. Is that better?" Ian Smith smirks.

"What if I don't want to go?" Antonio asks.

"It's not about desire, Antonio. It's about a divine

appointment. You are going one way or another. Think about Joseph and how he arrived at his destination." At the mouth of the alley stand two other men. "Bring Socrates to the car. Let's go," Ian Smith says to the men. The two grab Antonio by the arm and walk him to the car, a green vintage Bentley. A hand reaches out and opens the door. Antonio locks his knees to stop himself from being forced into the car.

"Oh, no, you don't!" one of the men says and shoves him into the car.

Ian Smith leans toward Antonio and whispers, "Don't resist. It's best to go along,"

Antonio glances at the side part in Ian Smith's fiery, slicked-back hair. He pulls his hoodie farther over his head. Silently, he prays, *All-Knowing, please escort me during this trip just as You escorted Joseph to get him where You needed him to be. May I be amenable to Your will. Please protect me. So be it.*

His thoughts turn to his sisters and aunt.

CHAPTER 6

BACK AT HOME

Alessandra, Aunt Ruth, and Maria are in the kitchen, drinking espresso. Standing at the sink and looking out the kitchen window, Alessandra laments, "We need to be prepared the next time there is a loud bang at the door and it's the U-Squad."

Aunt Ruth's tired eyes darken at Alessandra. "Here she goes talking about preparing for the U-Squad. Those people are dangerous! Exactly what would you suggest we do to 'prepare' for them?"

Opening a counter drawer, Alessandra pulls out a

pad and pencil. "We can surely put our dark-brown hairs together and create a plan. We can plan everything from the knock on the door to their leaving," Alessandra insists.

Aunt Ruth is impressed. "That might actually work," she says. "I'm in for anything that will ease my anxiousness during their horrible visits." Aunt Ruth finishes her espresso and goes to the espresso machine to make another.

Maria is bursting with excitement. "Write this down! Sell some of Mom and Dad's stuff to support Antonio. Have a ready answer to the questions they always ask."

"Yes, those are good, Maria. Also, we should remove or hide all documents and religious items from the house," Aunt Ruth adds.

"Let's keep going. This is helping to get my mind off the sadness in my heart," Alessandra says.

"Creating the list of what gets sold is a great way to continue. Place my teacup lamp on the list," Maria offers.

"The trunk in the attic will bring a good price. Mrs. Alfonsi has been asking about it ever since she was caught peeking in the window during one of our cleaning missions. Your grandmother and I emptied the trunk and had it put back into the attic," Aunt Ruth says while removing espresso cups from the table. "How about the old clock in the library? It's as imposing as a supervisor. Chiming every hour, reminding me that the days are short and are gone quickly."

"Not the library clock!" Alessandra shouts out of turn at Aunt Ruth. Aunt Ruth is taken aback. "Forgive me, Auntie. But it's sentimental. It has been in our family for years," Alessandra says, tempering her voice.

Aunt Ruth smiles. She walks over to Alessandra and gently touches her hand. "Sometimes I forget that I am your aunt by marriage. As much as I love this house, I still don't know all its stories," she says.

"My favorite memories are watching Dad pull out the boxes of decorations," Maria eagerly adds.

"He loved Christmas," Alessandra says, her mind aflush with warm memories. "Mother served hot cider as we all worked to turn this old house into a Christmas haven. It was so beautiful. I never wanted those times to end." Alessandra quickly wipes a tear from her eye.

Aunt Ruth puts her hand on Alessandra's shoulder. "Well, I vote to keep the Christmas stuff," she says.

CHAPTER 7

THE HIMERS INSTITUTE

The green Bentley stops in a garage. "Get out." Someone prods Antonio. Antonio is escorted to a private elevator.

"What are you looking at?" Ian Smith asks.

"There are only two buttons in the elevator, yet the building has at least thirteen floors," Antonio says.

"There are other things to think about," Ian Smith says. The door opens. "Let's go," Ian Smith says as he shoves Antonio forward.

Leaving the elevator, Antonio notices high ceilings, large windows, and luxurious marble floors. At the far end of the room, two men stand on either side of a high circular platform while another man, tall and thin, talks to another man on top of the platform. The tall man wears a black, double-breasted, pinstriped suit. His right sleeve has a burgundy ruffle from shoulder to wrist with gold thread running to the top edge of the ruffle.

Suddenly, the man talking to the tall man falls to the floor. The tall man turns to face the approaching group as two men whisk the fallen man away. Then suddenly two more men enter to take their place on either side of the platform. The tall man flickers a darkest gray shadow with horns and blue eyes, appearing as though the shadow is sharing his body.

Steady yourself, warns a voice inside Antonio. *He just slit that man's throat. Steady yourself. He who is with you is taller and stronger than this man. Pray for strength. It shall get worse than this.*

"It's not murder when you kill a clone ... or is it?" The tall man chuckles.

"Hello, Commander," Ian Smith says.

"Is it?" the commander repeats to Antonio. Antonio says nothing. The commander turns to a disturbed man standing away from the platform. The commander points at the frightened man. "That man can tell you it's better to kill the clone. As the original, his skills are hard to find. He's lucky. His unique skills keep him alive. Problem is, I just don't like him. And worse, that was my last clone," the commander says with feigned regret. "They take a dreadfully long time to make. You see, I am not killing a human being." The commander's eyes sparkle with dark glee.

Walking toward Antonio, the commander says, "You must be Antonio, whose parents either ran or collaborated with the resistance."

Ian Smith answers, "Yes, Commander. He is that Antonio."

"Are we friends, Ian?" the commander asks.

Ian Smith is speechless as fear floods his eyelids. "No, we are not! The boy can speak for himself!"

The commander scowls and leans in closer to Antonio. He and the flickering dark shadow with horns speak in unison. "I know who you are!"

Antonio recoils.

"Why is he not restrained?" the commander questions Ian Smith.

"He is just a boy, Commander," Ian Smith says confidently. "Look at him. He's harmless." Ian Smith slaps Antonio's back, and his lithe body plunges forward.

"His parents didn't command attention, yet they managed to organize and lead a revolt," the commander says. Peeling Antonio's hoodie to the back, he continues. "Are you like your parents, Antonio? Unassuming, seemingly weak, yet very dangerous?" the commander says, taunting Antonio.

Antonio remains silent, his face stern, every muscle in his body taut. The commander's eyes take in the boy.

He turns his back away from Antonio and snaps his left hand's fingers, styling long, golden nails.

How odd, Antonio thinks. The nails on the commander's right hand are short with no color. The left side of his hair is short and curled, while the right side falls straight, extending to his cheek bone. *What a mixed-up fellow*, Antonio muses.

"Well, that's enough killing for now. Take him away. Ian, I expect you to make sure he's restrained. Please. We don't want him getting away," the commander says.

Ian Smith roughly grab's Antonio's arm and takes him to a room with a metal door. Hearing the key turn in the lock, securing his capture in the white room, Antonio sits at an alabaster table in an alabaster chair. After seeing the murder of the clone and the demon shadowing the commander, he wonders whether he will escape alive.

Hours pass. Lulled by the whiteness of the room, Antonio falls into a deep sleep.

"Come join us," a voice calls to him. Antonio navigates

the white-clouded space with his hands extended in front of him. "Come join us," the voice calls again.

Antonio continues forward. "The All-Knowing has not given me a spirit of fear but a spirit of power," he coaches himself.

Entering a clearing, Antonio suddenly stands before the six kids the old man had told him about. "Where am I?" Antonio asks.

"You are in the Holy," answers a muscular, mahogany-skinned teen, his almond eyes revealing some Asian ancestry. "The Holy is a mental, cloudlike white space protected by an impenetrable, fine-gold spiritual mesh, actually an energy, that we can't see."

"We are safe here. The Anti-Knowing attempts to locate us, but the brightness of the Holy is an unapproachable light. I am Magus." Magus gleams.

Antonio notices a girl standing beside him, facing Magus along with him.

"I am Rita," the girl says to Magus. "I don't talk much, and I am not special."

Magus smiles knowingly. "Rita, though shy, you are special. Like all in the Holy, you answered this call for a reason. You were raised by survivalists. You are strong and capable of living off the grid. You can hunt, make a fire, build shelters, and get a prayer through in a hurry. Even your hair is dangerous. You are special and a force to be reckoned with, Rita."

She lowers her eyes, embarrassed but flattered. "Stop sharing my secrets." She smiles meekly. "But how? How do you know these things about me?" she asks in a petite voice. "I know nothing about you. But I know He who knows everything about everybody. The All-Knowing at His choosing shares information as needed to accomplish His will. I tend to listen more than most. Everyone here will eventually learn what your unique gifts are."

Rita's brows furrow in response.

"Take a closer look at the last gift your parents sent you," Magus says.

Antonio interrupts. "Who's the cool kid over there?" Antonio points to another boy in the Holy.

"I am Solomon. Friends call me 'Solo.' I tend to be an introvert," Solomon responds.

"Those are some 'instep' clothes you're wearing, real trendy," Antonio says. "I work at being instep."

"I know why I'm here. I am a technology savant. Well, actually, I hack networks, bypass firewalls, and enter back doors to gain information on enemy systems. My skills may come in handy," Solo says.

"How old are you?" Magus asks.

"Twelve," Solo returns.

"You look much older than twelve," Magus says. "Maybe it's your height. That may come in handy too."

"What enemy systems are you talking about?" Antonio asks.

Solo shrugs. "I was just showing off. I am twelve. What enemy systems do I know about? Mostly, I just enjoy building computers, searching corporate networks, and next-level gaming."

"You certainly don't seem like an introvert," says a brown-skinned boy with reddish-brown hair and dimples.

Solo turns toward the boy. "Who are you? You don't know me. I would know because I don't have many friends," Solo tells him.

"I am Jose. I am ten years old. My parents told me I was special, but I never understood what that meant. It felt good to hear it though."

"Antonio, meet Jose. His abilities far exceed the polygraph, injected truth serums, and torture. He is a great chess player." He points his finger up in the air. "Jose is an intuitive: able to accurately identify changes in emotion and temperament, and effectively read body language. Though because of his age, people who don't lean in miss who is standing in front of them and overrule him."

"How often are you correct?" Magus asks.

"One hundred percent of the time. I can read people and situations," Jose says with a smile that shows a tooth missing on the upper left side of his mouth.

Another boy steps forward in the line forming beside Antonio, Rita, and Solo in the clearing of the Holy. "I am

Garrett. I am a musician. I also sing or hum, especially when things get weird," he explains.

"He means when he gets scared," Solo says with a laugh.

Giving Solo the stink eye, Garrett continues. "Some of my songs have healing properties. It's amazing when that happens … on mission trips with my family primarily. My parents told me music is numerical, and certain sounds, when spoken, vibrate on a particular frequency and are carried through the atmosphere and are felt on some level by all. And since Magus is with us, he probably knows I wish I were a stronger, ruddier type."

"Strength comes in many forms," Antonio says. "Healing is an awesome power to have. Now, I am not psychic, but I believe that's going to very useful," Antonio says to Garrett. Magus smiles at this.

Another boy steps forward to introduce himself. "I am Michael. Having seen all manner of poverty and sickness, I wish to give back. My mother's family owned a small diamond mine prior to the war. I visited the mine twice and recall the poor treatment of the workers. My propensity to help others sometimes gets in the way of the mission, but I'm a giver and cannot help myself. I give my time, food, and—"

"Massages," Magus interrupts.

Everyone turns and stares quizzically at Michael. Solo breaks the awkward moment. "How will a 'giver' help us?" Solo asks.

"I never said I was a superhero. There is nothing special about me. I'm here to give what I can," Michael replies. Magus turns to Antonio.

"Introduce yourself, Antonio," Magus says to him.

Antonio steps forward with reluctance. "I am Antonio. I am—wait. How did this happen? What drew us here?" he asks.

Magus speaks up. "I have been sending messages to you from the Holy, but you didn't respond. When you met the commander, your fear spike created a black vapor within the spirit sphere. I saw it, traced its origin, and used the energy to draw us together here. Your capture is an appointed time in world history and eternity," Magus explains.

"What does his destiny have to do with me? I don't know any of you. Still unsure how I am here," Solo says.

"Antonio, you and Jose are asleep. Rita, Dietrich, and Michael have open minds, making it easy to communicate with them, and I am meditating on the All-Knowing," Magus replies.

"An appointed time? If I am dreaming, when I wake up, there's a cross-dressing clone killer waiting to 'meet' me!" Antonio's fear spikes.

"Do calm yourself," Magus says. "We are safe here in the Holy, and you are not exactly dreaming. You are 'seeing.' What have you been told of what is going on?"

"What I have been told by a wise man is that our parents served as members of an organization that fought by organizing people and creating campaigns to get the word out about the All-Knowing," Antonio informs the group of young people. "The government permanently silenced our parents for their relationship with the

All-Knowing. Knowing the All-Knowing made them confident and secure, even when they counted the cost."

"Living on a fearless plain made them dangerous," Magus says. Stepping forward, he continues, "Each of you are special."

"Antonio, they are coming for you!" Jose alerts him. Antonio is alarmed.

"You must stay asleep," Jose continues.

"Who is coming for me?" Antonio asks.

"The man with the orange hair is coming for you," Jose tells Antonio.

"How do I stay asleep?" Antonio asks.

"When they try to wake you, stay here in the Holy," Magus assures.

"What do we do?" Rita asks. "Will they come for us too? I am not ready for this. My parents were believers in the All-Knowing. I mean, I believe but not like them. Who will protect us?" she asks with concern.

"Duh!" Solo blurts. "Guardian angels!"

"We have guardian angels?" Jose asks excitedly. "I have a guardian angel? What does my angel look like?"

"Your angel looks like you. Remember when an angel freed Peter from jail. He then went to the house where the other believers were staying. Rhoda answered the door and informed the occupants that Peter's angel was at the door. You see, it wasn't an angel. It was Peter. That's how I know our Guardians looks like us," Dietrich explains wisely.

Rita sits down and asks, "Guardian angel? Meaning we are in danger?"

"Yes, we are, Rita," Antonio says. "We are in danger. This is not a dream, though it feels dreamish but better. My fear meter is lower in the Holy. However, they will come for me."

"Will Antonio's guardian angel protect him?" Rita asks.

"I'm not exactly sure how that works," Magus responds.

Antonio offers some hope. "What I know is that the underground network is destroyed without leadership. I'm not sure if we are up to this. I didn't volunteer, but I am accepting the call, and I think we all should."

Antonio hears footsteps in the corridor outside his room. Antonio's sleeping body stays still while his mind is far off in the Holy.

"Antonio, they are upon you! Stay with us. Maybe they will go away if they can't wake you," Jose exclaims.

Magus stands in the center of the Holy. He looks at them all. "If you are not in, now's the time to say so," Magus tells them.

The sound of a key turning the door lock steals Antonio's attention. His shaking body breaks his concentration and pulls him from the Holy.

"Wake him up at once!" Ian Smith yells.

"I am trying. He's sleeping hard, sir," one of the guards says.

Ian Smith walks over and lands a powerful fist upon Antonio's head. Antonio doesn't respond.

"I can't hang on much longer," Antonio cries to his new

friends in the Holy. "Magus, keep us together!" Antonio shouts as he concentrates, struggling between two worlds.

"Hold on, Antonio!" Magus exclaims.

"He's punching me. Ugh!" Antonio struggles to say.

"Your gifts are unique. Use the *power* daily!" Magus yells.

"Ugh!" Antonio moans in pain.

"Remember your power of prayer, Antonio, and quickly!" Magus encourages.

On the other side, Ian Smith is enraged. "Wake up, or I will shoot you," he hisses through clenched teeth.

Antonio leaves the Holy, and his mind returns to his alabaster cell.

"Sleeping deeply, princess?" Ian Smith asks rhetorically. "The commander wants to see you. And he's not in a good mood. You better have some answers, young Antonio," he says joyfully as one of the guards wrenches him to his feet.

Working to focus his sight and to hear above the throbbing pain in his left ear, Antonio lumbers through the corridor, escorted by Ian Smith and other degenerates.

Antonio wonders how the All-Knowing will get him out of this. Confidence wells up in him.

How strange, he thinks.

He mumbles, "B—H—B."

"What did you say?" Ian Smith asks.

"B—H—B," Antonio responds, his voice rising.

"I think I hit you too hard. You are talking gibberish." Ian Smith laughs.

"The battle has begun," Antonio mutters.

"For your sake, Antonio, I hope not. You and your friends could get badly hurt." Ian Smith smirks.

Antonio snaps his head to look, wondering how Ian Smith could know about the others.

ABOUT THE AUTHOR

Lindsay Brown is an energetic and engaging Christian writer and speaker. She grew up on the South Side of Chicago where most days were spent looking out of her kitchen window dreaming of the journeys and adventures she read about. On Saturday mornings, in 6th grade, she competed on the radio show "The Battle of the Books". The battle was to correctly answer more questions related to Newberry Award Winner books than the competing school. At the age of 13, her poem The 13th Floor was published by the University of Illinois at Circle Campus press. This was just the beginning Lindsay continued to write short stories and articles. Her book Sunshine Why Would You Do That?, consists of stories of Christian women misbehaving in relationships. She is currently working on her second book in the Sunshine Why Would You Do That? series "Bad Actors in the workplace."

During an early morning summer walk, twenty years ago, the story Armed without Bibles wafted into her mind. The story was shelved until she picked it up again and realized the year 2020 is when the story starts.

Lindsay is a professional member of the National Speakers Association. She holds a degree in Communications, North Central College. She has three children who love her and lives grateful for each day with her husband the love of her life.

Lightning Source UK Ltd.
Milton Keynes UK
UKHW012252250920
370551UK00002B/60/J